Date Due

CONS, **EH?**

Sir John, Eh?
Used to drink a bottle a day,
Thereby proving to Viscount Monck
That the only way to govern Canada was drunk.

CONSERVE TUVS, EH?

ILLUSTRATION BY
ISAAC BICKERSTAFF

TEXT BY
MARK M. ORKIN

Stoddart

First published in 1986 by
Stoddart Publishing Co. Limited
34 Lesmill Road
Toronto, Canada
M3B 2T6

Canadian Cataloguing in Publication Data

Orkin, Mark M.
    Conserve Tuvs, Eh?

ISBN 0-7737-5077-0

1. Canada-Politics and government- 1984-
-Anecdotes, facetiae, satire, etc.* 2. Progressive Conservative Party of Canada -Anecdotes, facetiae, satire, etc. I. Bickerstaff, Isaac II. Title.

FC630.075 1986   971.064'7'0207   C86-093969-3
F1034.2.075 1986

DESIGN: Brant Cowie/Artplus Ltd.

Printed and bound in Canada by John Deyell Company

OTHER BOOKS

BY MARK M. ORKIN
HUMOR
Canajan, Eh?
French Canajan, Hé?
Murrican, Huh?

LANGUAGE
Speaking Canadian English
Speaking Canadian French

OTHER
Sex Wars
The Great Stork Derby

LAW
Legal Ethics
The Law of Costs

BY ISAAC BICKERSTAFF
Mariposa Forever
Friends, Hosers & Countrymen
What's the Difference?

A New Ministry

Prime Minister Brian Mulroney made the House of Commons sit up and take notice the other day.

In one of his rare appearances during Question Period, the P.M. announced the creation of a new Ministry. Addressing the House from the Speaker's chair to demonstrate that he is all things to all men and in the absence of the Speaker, Mr. John Bosley, who was away attending the official opening of the Roman baths at his Meech Lake villa, the P.M. spoke in moving terms of the fulfilment of a long-standing dream.

Ever since his days as a *'tit gars* playing hockey with a frozen road-apple on the streets of Baie Comeau, Mr. Mulroney recounted, he had dreamed of leaving his mark on Canada. Earlier achievements such as shutting down the Iron Ore Company operations at Shefferville or euchreing Joe Clark out of the party leadership had been no more than trial runs at his lifelong ambition. They had left their mark on the workers of Shefferville and Joe Clark, respectively, but he had something more significant in mind.

To a standing ovation from the government benches, Mr. Mulroney proudly announced the creation of a Ministry of Sacred Trusts. The idea had come to him, he said, as a result of attempts by Finance Minister Michael Wilson to de-index old-age pensions. Only then had he realized for the first time that sacred trusts could not be left to take care of themselves. Someone had to make sure they remained both sacred and trusty. That's where his administration with its policy of openness in government and an end to political patronage came in. One could always count on the Conserve Tuvs and their appointees to detect and preserve sacred trusts, he added.

The department would be a small one, Mr. Mulroney emphasized, brushing aside Opposition concerns about increasing the Federal deficit, the reduction of which his party considered a sacred trust. It would be housed, he added, in one of the temporary buildings that had been erected during World War II on Wellington Street West, a.k.a. the Street of Broken Dreams. The building was, of course, temporary, but then so were most sacred trusts.

Mr. Mulroney left the House immediately after making the brief announcement. His press secretary told a crowd of waiting television reporters that the P.M. was already late for a recording session at a local studio where he had arranged to do a videotape of "When Yiddish Eyes Are Smiling," to be aired on Yom Kippur at Toronto's Holy Bosom Temple. He would, however, be making a full statement to the Canajan people about the new Ministry during his next Christmas message, for which Her Majesty the Queen had graciously permitted herself to be pre-empted.

Opposition Leader John Turner, who had been trying for ten minutes to catch the TV cameraman's eye, denounced what he called Mr. Mulroney's blatant grab for the ethnic vote. His embroidered yarmulke pushed well back on his head, his blue eyes blazing, his forefinger stabbing the air repeatedly, Mr. Turner charged the P.M. with barefaced theft of Liberal property, to wit, the Jewish vote which had belonged to his party ever since people had forgotten how Mackenzie King refused admission to refugees from Nazi persecution during the Thirties. "Jews, if necessary," the great Liberal statesman had remarked at the time with the slight lisp of the born orator, "but not necessarily Jews."

Meanwhile, back at the House, Deputy Prime Minister Don Mazankowski promised to set aside fifteen minutes later in the session for a full debate on the new Ministry.

Monkey Business

Every Canajan political leader has had a distinctive symbol— a whisky bottle, a rose, a banana, whatever.

After a long period of trial and error, Brian Mulroney has found his very own symbol that he shares with only a few close friends— three brass monkeys. Their motto: see no evil, speak no evil, hear no evil.

As the top monkey, the P.M. stays away from the House of Commons as much as possible and spends the rest of the time with both hands pressed firmly over his eyes. That way he never sees anything bad about his ministers.

Rotten tuna? "Didn't see a thing, but when I got wind of it, Bang!"

The travels of Suzanne? "Didn't see a thing, but when the bill from Visa came in, Bang!"

The P.M.'s former Number Two monkey, Erik ("Velcro-lips") Nielsen, had but one answer to every attack on cabinet colleagues.

"Who, *me* listening at the Grits' keyhole? I have nothing to say." Andrée Champagne's letter about buying young Conserve Tuvs with taxpayers' money? "I have nothing to say."

Add to them Sinclair Stevens as third monkey. Like husbands everywhere he goes through life with both hands over his ears.

"Sinc!"

"Mm-m."

"Are you asleep?"

"What is it, Noreen?"

"I've something to tell you."

"Your headache's better?"

"No, silly. It's about borrowing—"

"Noreen! Are you trying to tell me about my blind trust again?"

"But Sinkie, I've got to talk to *someone* about it."

"Not to me, you don't. Where the dickens is that little black box that Brian gave me for Christmas? Oh, here it is."

"But Sinc, I just *had* to find 2.6 million dol— *(bleep!)* somewhere. *(Bleep!)* said he was a bit short that week so he sent me to *(bleep!)* and *he* agreed to lend us the money interest fr— *(bleep! bleep! bleep!)*. SINCLAIR! Will you put that damn toy away and listen to me!!"

Well, that's how the trio managed to hold off the combined Opposition for two weeks. The P.M. was in China and hadn't seen anything. Erik Nielsen wouldn't say anything. And Sinclair Stevens hadn't heard anything. It was a triple play that made Tinkers-to-Evers-to-Chance look like bush-leaguers.

Of course, the buck had to stop sometime. Two point six million bucks, in fact. The buck stopped when the beleaguered Industry Minister joined a gaggle of earlier cabinet ministers at the bottom of the deep blue.

It's a funny thing about the Conserve Tuvs. The biggest parliamentary majority in history and they're out of Sinc.

Banks You Can't Bank on Anymore

The long love-in between Canajans and their banks has gone phfft!

Things didn't used to be like that B.C., Before the Conserve Tuvs, that is. Way back then Canajans had this real pash for banks because they were so big. So strong. So *banky*. At the same time they were ever so soft and feminine: Mary smiling her shy, warm smile at the Royal; Anne Murray crooning Country and Western over at the Commerce. A chorus line of young women at the counter were eager to take our money and send us on our way with a cheery "Have a good day!" They made us feel really comfy about our overdraft.

Not any more. First off, management introduced cold, impersonal banking machines between Canajans and the object of their affections. Who can make love to an Instant Teller? Next thing, any young women who hadn't been automated were always too busy to spend time with the customers. They used to leave us standing at the wicket like fools while they worked on their shopping lists. Instead of "Have a nice day," they put us off with a triumphant "Sorry, our computers are down this morning." Or else they handed us back our passbook with a dismissive "There you go!"

What happened to Canajan banking?

For years Mr. Mulroney went around telling everyone who would listen how twenty years of Liberal mismanagement had left the economy looking like a Swiss cheese. As a result, he says, the country is broke, bankrupt, busted. Well, maybe he's right, although when Mary and Anne were in charge of things back in good old B.C. the banks looked to be in great shape. In those days the Inspector-General of Banks didn't have to go around wearing a Smile button in his lapel.

10

During the last election campaign Mr. Mulroney went around promising to stop up the holes in the cheese with massive injections of capital. That was supposed to end the Emmenthal effect forever and produce, in his oft-repeated phrase, jobs, jobs, jobs.

Well, Barbara McDougall, the late Minister of State for Finance, certainly did a job on Canajans who are beginning to realize what the P.M.'s phrase meant. Never mind twenty years of Liberal mismanagement; in a few short months of Conserve Tuv management Barbara undid all the good work of Mary and Anne. Suddenly banks were falling like dandruff on a credit manager's shoulder.

Why is this? Well, for starters, Barbara's TV commercials were simply terrible. Where Anne and Mary cooed and wooed, Barbara scared the pants off the viewers. Any account executive worth his residuals could have told her that you can't frighten people into buying the product. "I don't apologize for trying to save the Canadian Commercial Bank," she announced fiercely, although no one had asked her to. "This isn't going to be cheap," she warned us with a menacing look as we subconsciously slipped one hand in our pocket to make sure our wallet was still there. Anyway, neither Anne nor Mary would ever have made the mistake of going on camera flanked by Gerald Bouey of all people. *Bad* vibes. With those TV commercials should anyone be surprised that consumer confidence is in the basement?

And then, the way the former Minister of State for Finance airily promised to throw a billion dollars of our hard-earned into the bailout made one long for those good old B.C. days when C. D. Howe tried to silence the Opposition during the Great Pipeline Debate with the quip "What's a million?" and succeeded in blowing an election. Barbara made old C. D. look like a piker.

It's going to be a long time, though, before anyone in Canada makes love to a bank again.

Dirty Pool

Sussex Drive watchers are wondering why there has been no mention of the swimming pool at No. 24 since Mr. Mulroney became prime minister.

The pool had been donated to Pierre Trudeau during his term as P.M. by a group of anonymous well-wishers, an act that drove media people wild. In those days rarely a week went by without some picky reference to the gift and its unknown donors. But when Mr. Mulroney took office all references to the swimming pool stopped, apparently on orders from the PMO. Only now is the explanation coming to light.

For months personnel of the new Security Service had been combing the P.M.'s residence, but Mr. Mulroney regularly dismissed reporters' questions with an airy "Nothing for you today, boys." When questioned about what the security people were combing for, he would only say, "Oh, just getting some of the tangles out. You know the mess the Liberals left things in."

Privately, though, Mr. Mulroney was as mystified as everyone else.

"Mila, my dear, there's something I've been meaning to ask you."

"Yes, Brian?"

"What I have to say is *very* confidential. For your ears only. Hush-hush, in fact. *Pas devant les domestiques*, if you get my meaning."

"Oh, that's all right, Brian, the cleaning lady just left. I'm going to have trouble with her, though. Now that Angelinha is learning English she wants more money. She says that her girlfriend Maria who works for Geills is making minimum wage and . . ."

"Never mind that now, my dear. This is important. Have you seen the swimming pool lately?"

"I don't think so, Brian. Where did you leave it?"

"That's the problem, Mila. I can't find it anywhere."

"Well, I could ask Angelinha next Wednesday if you like."

"No, no, my dear. I don't want anything said about it. You remember how the media went after Joe when he lost his luggage. Can you imagine what would happen if they found out that I'd mislaid a swimming pool?"

"That could be bad, Brian?"

"After what I've called *them*, Mila, those effete media snobs would cut out my liver and eat it for breakfast."

As a result of the recent security sweep, however, the truth has come out. It appears that when Mr. Trudeau resigned as prime minister and left 24 Sussex Drive for private life in Montreal, he took the swimming pool with him.

The loss was discovered shortly after the Turners moved in. When Senator Keith Davey was enlisted to help salvage the floundering 1984 election campaign, he ordered the pool filled with hot water, hoping that Mr. Turner would feel more natural that way, but his gofer reported that the pool was not in its usual place. Before anything could be done to retrieve either the pool or the campaign, however, Mr. Turner found himself preoccupied with picking out new wallpaper for Stornoway. When asked by then Clerk of the Privy Council, Gordon Osbaldeston, whether the incoming prime minister should be briefed on the missing pool Mr. Turner snarled, "Let Mulroney worry about it."

Now it is indeed Mr. Mulroney who must worry about it. And as usual with affairs of state there are no easy answers. If he insists on Mr. Trudeau's returning the pool, Mr. Mulroney risks alienating Quebeckers just at a time when he is trying to bring their province into the constitutional accord. If he does nothing the West will accuse him of being soft on the Frenchies. Meanwhile, feelings are running high. A usually reliable source reports that Elizabeth Gray was fired from *As It Happens* only hours before she planned to air a live interview with the plumber who disconnected the pool.

According to a Canajan Press report which has been denied by the PMO, the Mulroneys just discovered that when Mr. Trudeau vacated 24 Sussex Drive, he also removed the toilet.

Nepotism's My Ism Son, What's Yours?

Former Justice Minister John Crosbie was justifiably irked at being accused in the House of Commons of engaging in nepotism.

Everybody in the outports, he announced with some heat, knows that nepotism derives from the Latin word for nephew and means finding a job for your sister's *schlemiel* of a son who couldn't do an honest day's work if he stood on his head when he doesn't even have one to stand on in the first place.

He himself, he assured the House, wouldn't dream of doing such a thing and wanted it on the public record that he had never tried to benefit his sister's kids at public expense in his whole life, other than getting them on the welfare rolls which every clean-living Newfoundland citizen is entitled to anyway. There was not, he insisted, a jot or tittle of evidence to the contrary.

In response to catcalls and Opposition cries of "What about Michael and Ches?" he acknowledged that, yes, he *had* thrown a few jots and tittles of government work to two struggling young lawyers in St. John's who just happened to share his name and what was wrong with that? It certainly wasn't nepotism in the strictly legal sense because they weren't his nephews and that's what counts among lawyers. Besides, any minister of justice who refused to steer a little legal business to his own sons didn't deserve to be remembered with a card on Father's Day.

With the Opposition in no mood to let him off the hook of his own devising, Mr. Crosbie was goaded into an uncharacteristic *ad hominem* response, calling one of his parliamentary attackers a sleaze-bag. The Canajan Press has consulted several eminent scholars at St. John's Memorial U. who advise that sleaze-bag is a Newfoundland version of the more familiar gutter term "scum-bag."

Outside the House, Mr. Crosbie told reporters that although he first encountered the term scum-bag while studying gutter law at Harvard he had not used it in debate for fear of giving offence to his constituents in the little outport of Scum Bag Chance. Besides, he said, there was no need for Newfoundlanders to borrow gutter terms from the mainland since they already had enough of their own.

Stinking Fish

For some time old Ottawa hands have noticed an unusually strong smell emanating from Parliament Hill.

Its source remains in doubt. Some observers felt that it came from the recently established Ministry of Sacred Trusts whose refrigeration facilities had not yet been installed because of budgetary restraints. Others suggested that the odor was caused by Mr. Mulroney's decomposing campaign promises.

When these and other theories about the smell were raised during Question Period, Erik Nielsen, speaking for an absent Prime Minister, replied with his accustomed sense of fair play that it probably came from the N.D.P.'s dead hopes of ever attaining power. At this Mr. Ed Broadbent was seen to shake his head vigorously, while holding a handkerchief to his nose and gesturing in the direction of the Liberal benches.

House of Commons staff have now traced down the source of the smell, which is indeed political. It appears that shopkeepers who removed a million cans of rancid and decomposing tuna from shelves across the country had forwarded them in protest to former Fisheries Minister John Fraser. Although his own department's inspectors earlier had found the fish unfit for human consumption, Mr. Fraser ordered sales to proceed in order to protect the New Brunswick firm that processed the stuff in the first place. The tuna was both nourishing and safe to eat, Mr. Fraser assured a CBC interviewer the day before he resigned, although he declined to eat some of it himself when it was offered, pleading a prior dinner engagement.

New Brunswick Premier Richard Hatfield, a recognized authority on stinking fish, ordered a can tested by a provincial agency which later reported that parts of it were not bad at all.

The Premier plans to serve tuna casserole at his next b.y.o.b. party.

Incest Begins at Home

The Prime Minister is getting the state back into the bedrooms of the nation.

In so doing, Mr. Mulroney has reversed a process begun by Pierre Trudeau more than a decade ago.

It seems that the P.M. is becoming increasingly sensitive to media criticism, particularly from members of the parliamentary press gallery whose constant reminders of promises broken and patronage strewn about like confetti have been getting under the prime ministerial epidermis of late.

In a recent interview Mr. Mulroney, who is nothing if not fair-minded, disclaimed any suggestion of malice on the part of the offending journalists. "I think," he told Peter Gzowski, more in anger than in sorrow, "it is just the fact of so much intellectual incest taking place here in Ottawa."

With the best will in the world the P.M. has put his finger on a very sensitive spot. No one, least of all Ottawans whose moral rectitude has always been beyond question, likes to be accused on network radio of what has been called the last taboo. The fact that the P.M. spoke of the intellectual variety has not reassured concerned citizens who fear a witch-hunt. It is understood that the director of the Canadian Civil Liberties Association has asked CBC for equal air time to respond.

Whether Mr. Mulroney's remark is no more than the latest example of his penchant for hyperbole remains to be seen, but it has Ottawa swingers worried.

Losers Can Be Finders

External Affairs Minister Joe Clark may have finally broken his habit of losing things.

At various times in the past the former P.M. has managed to lose his luggage, the capital of Israel, a federal election, the prime ministership and the leadership of his party, roughly in that order.

But times change and Mr. Clark has now begun finding things. Not long ago he found government jobs for his brother as legal counsel for the 1988 Calgary Olympics and for his sister-in-law on the National Parole Board.

This could be the start of a trend.

GOOD NEWS, DARLING: I FOUND YOUR HEAD. THE CAT WAS PLAYING WITH IT.

Back up, Canada–I

Brian Mulroney has introduced a new posture into Canajan politics. Some people would say that it's about time.

In the past our prime ministers have always believed that position is everything in life and they are remembered as much for their postures as for their mottos. Some of these are almost too well known to require mention. For example:

Sir John, Eh? Posture: a bent elbow. Motto: "Here's to ye', laddie!"

Sir Wilfrid Laurier. Posture: a faraway look in the eye. Motto: "Didn't I see the Twentieth Century out there someplace?"

Mike Pearson. Posture: survival stance. Motto: "I'd rather be Pink than stink."

Joe Clark. Posture: just looking. Motto: "Now where the dickens did I put that . . . Maureeeeeeen!"

John Turner. Posture: defiance. Motto: "I may pat, but I'm no patsy!"

Brian Mulroney. Posture: hands held up in a gesture of sweet reasonableness. Motto: "Back up, fellows!"

The Mulroney posture may prove to be the best one of all. Earlier Conserve Tuv leaders like John Diefenbaker and Joe Clark were fond of using their own feet for target practice. Trouble was, the better the aim the worse off the marksman. Now Mr. Mulroney has gone them one better. By backing away from his self-inflicted wounds, he can claim to be cured.

Already observers are calling it the wonder drug of the Eighties.

Back up, Canada-II

By introducing the automatic transmission to Parliament, Mr. Mulroney has been able to reverse himself smoothly in the face of aroused public opposition. He now solves the most difficult problems by first creating and then backing away from them. Item: the proposal to eliminate universality in social programs. The solution: "Hey, hold on a minute, it was only one of a number of options for discussion. Back up, fellows."

Item: the proposal to de-index old-age pensions. The solution: "Hey, hold on a minute, those old buggers have a vote. Back up, fellows."

Item: free trade with the U.S. The solution: "Hey, hold on a minute, what I really meant was *freer* trade. Back up, fellows."

Item: the stinking tuna caper. The solution: "Phew! back up, fellows!"

Mr. Mulroney's ability to move backwards without tripping over his own or someone else's feet has been attributed to his lifelong admiration for the great Canajan statesman, Mackenzie King, but in fact the truth lies in the P.M.'s own boyhood.

When he was still a '*tit gars*, the young Brian Mulroney read an ad in the Baie Comeau weekly paper that, along with other novelties, offered for sale the "See-Back-o-Scope," a device which, when held up to the eye, permitted the viewer to look backward while facing forward ("See what's going on behind your back! Surprise your friends!"). Resisting the temptation to purchase a "Poo-poo Pillow" from the same source instead ("Place it under a seat cushion and wait for someone to sit down. Surprise your friends!"), little Brian sent off his weekly allowance of fifty cents to the Johnson Company in Racine, Wisconsin.

It proved to be a decision that changed his life. Some weeks later when a small parcel arrived at the Mulroney residence, young Brian retired at once to the family bathroom where he spent hours perfecting his skills with the See-Back-o-Scope. In no time he had developed the uncanny ability to walk backwards while confidently facing forward that would later see him safely through every self-induced crisis.

It is an ability that surprised not only his friends, as the ad had promised, but also the nation.

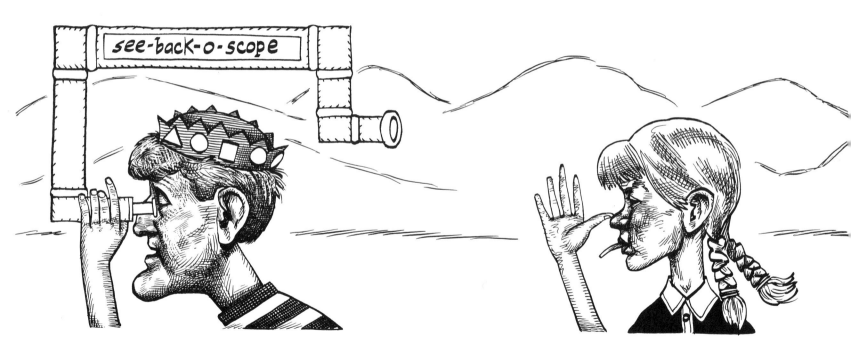

I'd Rather Be Prime Minister than Right

The first article of Canajan political faith has always been the doctrine of prime ministerial infallibility.

Historically, the pattern was set by the great Liberal statesman, Mackenzie King who, following the example of Sir John, Eh?, always consulted the spirits for guidance. Conserve Tuv leaders likewise cleared things with a higher source. Several of them, indeed, came to believe that they *were* the Higher Source.

That is why political observers were astounded not long ago when Mr. Mulroney publicly disclaimed divine insight. It was the first time this had happened in Canajan politics since 1922 when Arthur Meighen winged it and blew the King-Byng thing.

In fairness to Mr. Mulroney, he had been sorely pressed by events of his own making. The collapse of the Canadian Commercial Bank had caused a firestorm across the country. For seven straight days the Opposition parties had hammered him in the Commons for his decision to go for a half-billion dollar bailout package for the bank rather than deep-six it when even the cat could have seen that it was dead in the water.

Mr. Mulroney retorted with some exasperation that his decision had been based on all the facts that were available at the time. Then he dropped the clanger. "With the possible exception of the Blessed Virgin Mary," he told the House, "nobody can know the future with certainty. All we knew was that there was a problem. It was dealt with seriously."

The disclosure that the P.M. acted in such a serious matter without divine guidance may prove more damaging to the Conserve Tuvs in the long run than the long run on the Canadian Commercial Bank that followed the bailout. With his admission Mr. Mulroney shattered a doctrine upon which Canajan parliamentary democracy has rested since the days of Sir John, Eh?

Canajans now see, for the first time, that although by constitutional convention all prime ministers are infallible, some are less infallible than others. It is a thought that will take getting used to.

Day Care, Who Care

Canajan women never had it so good as under the Conserve Tuvs.

Well, not equal pay for work of equal value — that'll take a little time. And not a strong spokesperson for women in the PMO — it's too early for that yet. And certainly not censuring parliamentary wife-beaters — come on, that's a private matter, eh?

Not to worry. The Conserve Tuvs have launched a pilot project for fully funded day care that, if extended, should enable millions of working mothers to achieve their full potential.

Appropriately enough, the project was announced by Mila Mulroney, the Prime Minister's wife and a working mother. According to the Canajan Press, Ms. Mulroney "has her own small staff and office suite in the Prime Minister's complex of offices across the street from Parliament Hill." It is there that a day care centre has been installed for the newest Mulroney baby, wee Nicolas. But let an ecstatic Ms. Mulroney explain in her own words how the system works. "I look forward to having a playpen in the office," she told a *Canada AM* interviewer. "I think many working mothers do that and I'm going to enjoy every bit of time I can spend with him."

The news was received with enthusiasm by mothers across the country, although some business groups expressed reservations. With office rentals running in the twenty to forty dollars a square foot range, many employers are not sure where to put all those playpens. Meantime, former Minister of Employment and Immigration Flora MacDonald had ordered a feasibility study.

Patience, working mothers, help is on the way!

Cronyism Is My Ism, Pal; What's Yours?

When John Crosbie was accused of nepotism some time ago, Prime Minister Mulroney sprang to his defence even as the tiger springs to protect its cubs.

Denying charges that his Justice Minister had behaved improperly by steering government legal business to his two lawyer sons, Mr. Mulroney assured the House that, speaking as a lawyer, he saw nothing illegal, immoral or fattening about the practice and anyone who thought otherwise had a dirty mind. Besides, he added, in the deep, measured tones that he reserves for solemn avowals, "Mr. Crosbie is a most honorable man."

Mr. Crosbie, flushed from his own verbal jousts with Opposition members, was seen to nod vigorously in agreement with his leader's tribute.

Some time later Mr. Mulroney himself came under attack when John Turner levelled charges of cronyism against the Prime Minister.

Cronyism—the conferring of rewards on one's cronies—is an ancient prerogative of government ministers, the P.M. being, by virtue of his office, first in line when it comes to handing out the goodies. Since the word crony derives from the Greek *kronios*, meaning ancient, by tradition one's oldest friends get the fattest rewards.

In the present case the fat reward was a lucrative contract for government legal work, and the crony was a lawyer and old roommate of the P.M.'s from his student days at St. Francis Xavier University in Nova Scotia. According to Mr. Turner, also a lawyer, the crony peddled the contract to several law firms in the high-rent district before striking a deal with the one that offered him the best deal.

While Mr. Mulroney was busy defending himself, the crony, the law firm and the practice of peddling government goodies, Mr. Crosbie—also a lawyer—sat unusually silent. This has some observers wondering whether there is a rift in the loot.

Promises, Promises

The Prime Minister rejects Opposition charges that his government has done nothing to reduce the deficit since taking office in 1984. By not fulfilling his campaign promises he has saved the country hundreds of millions of dollars that might otherwise have been wasted. Despite strong pressure from the unemployed, farmers, fishermen, women and other malcontents, Mr. Mulroney resisted the temptation to keep his word and the country is the richer for it.

Honor Bright

Things have been rather quiet lately over at the new federal Ministry of Sacred Trusts.

This should come as no surprise in light of a recently leaked cabinet document reporting a steady decline in the number of sacred trusts under administration.

One-time Industry Minister Sinclair Stevens, a frequent critic of the sacred trusts lobby, has always seemed unconcerned. Interviewed at Ottawa's Upland Airport the other day as he was boarding a Government jet for a quick trip to Toronto to pick up his shirts from the laundry, he told TV reporters: "In a time of—uh—financial restraint, the country may well have to forgo the—uh—luxury of sacred trusts."

Meanwhile, officials at the new Ministry were left twiddling their thumbs when the Prime Minister appointed a task force to find something for them to do.

So far, Mr. Mulroney has rejected out of hand a suggestion from the Liberal rat pack that the new Ministry take charge of the flight logs of the Government's executive jet fleet which the P.M. once light-heartedly referred to as "sacred instruments of travel."

Another suggestion being given serious consideration by the task force is to have the Ministry of Sacred Trusts take over responsibility for parliamentary honor.

As recent events have made clear, parliamentary honor may be wearing thin in spots and the thought is that the Ministry of Sacred Trusts might store and recondition it.

The problem is particularly acute among former cabinet ministers. First, Defence Minister Robert Coates resigned after visiting a West German sex club, despite the P.M.'s assurances in the House that Mr. Coates was an honorable man who had done the honorable thing. Then Fisheries Minister John Fraser resigned after flooding

the country with a million tins of tainted tuna and the P.M. was obliged to read the same statement again in which Mr. Coates's name had been crossed out and Mr. Fraser's name pencilled in. The same statement was trotted out for Communications Minister Marcel Masse and, by now slightly dog-eared, for Industry Minister Sinclair Stevens.

Nor is the problem confined to former ministers. When Mr. Crosbie was charged with committing nepotism (which is not, he reminded the House, an indictable offence in his native Newfoundland), Mr. Mulroney treated the House to a re-run of the Coates script only this time substituting Mr. Crosbie's name.

Now people are saying that this is not good enough. They point out that, at present, members of Parliament entering the House can check their hats, coats and galoshes. The Ministry of Sacred Trusts, they say, could provide a convenient place to check their honor.

Mila and the Horsemen

While their husbands were discussing affairs of state at the Shamrock Summit in Quebec City, Nancy Reagan and Mila Mulroney visited together.

They talked about a wide range of women's issues: the children; where to buy shoes; the importance of serving a hot breakfast before their husbands went off to work; and where Nancy sold her designer dresses after she'd worn them once. As they compared notes, Nancy was astounded to learn that R.C.M.P. personnel on duty at 24 Sussex Drive kept their hands in their pockets whenever Mila went by.

"Mila!" she exclaimed, "you mean to tell me those cowboys in the pointy hats don't salute you?"

"Well, no. Should they?"

"I'll say! Back home at the White House everybody salutes *me!* "

"How's that?"

"Because my Ron is President with a capital pee and that makes me First Lady. The doormen salute me, or else!"

"But— but here they're not doormen, they're the Royal Canadian Mounted Police."

"Doormen, horsemen, what's the difference. I'll tell you something, Mila; I spoke to my Ron about it right at the beginning and he told me: 'If they don't salute, sweetheart, I'll have someone sent over from Central Casting who will.' There's been no trouble ever since."

Later that day, Mila confronted her husband alone.

"Brian?"

"Yes, Mila."

"I want to ask you something."

"Will it keep, Mila? I'm already late for an appointment with my voice coach. We're still having trouble with the second chorus of

'When Irish Eyes Are Smiling' and I want to work on it. Mi—mi
—mi!"

"Well, it's just that Nancy Reagan says the Mounties should salute me. I told her that whenever I see a policeman I feel like saluting *him* and she looked at me as though I just got off the boat. Am I doing something wrong?"

"Not at all, my dear. When I was a *'tit gars* in Baie Comeau we always saluted the police too. How many fingers did *you* use?"

"Brian, please try to be serious; this isn't the House of Commons. I don't want people to think I'm still an immigrant."

"Mila, you've given me a great idea! If I tell that little story at my next press conference the ethnics will eat it up. We'll steal half a million votes from the Grits!"

"But Brian—"

"Sorry, my dear, Signora Parmegiano is waiting for me. But don't worry your pretty head about it, sweetheart. I'll talk to the Commissioner as soon as we get home."

Bottoms Up

The Prime Minister issued a challenge a while ago that has Ottawa guessing.

Stung by suggestions that he may have told less than the truth about the tainted tuna caper, Mr. Mulroney offered to put his seat on the line if those who doubted his word would do the same. Members of Parliament, although impressed, were puzzled.

All the world loves a fighter, but this was something new. Not even the oldest free-loader in the parliamentary restaurant could recall having heard such a challenge before and no one knew what to make of it. What would happen after everyone put his seat on the line? If their seats were on the line how could they stand for re-election? Who would decide on the winner? What were the rules? It all sounded very uncomfortable.

Members who consulted Beauchesne's bible of parliamentary procedure could find nothing in the index under either "seat" or "line."

Other members spoke to former M.P. Stanley Knowles who knows the rules backwards, a rare accomplishment these days. Scratching the side of his jaw with his left thumb, Mr. Knowles recalled that when he was a lad in Winnipeg boys challenged each other by drawing a line on the ground and daring the other boy to step over it. Perhaps, he suggested, *'tit gars* in Baie Comeau used to put their seats on the line instead, although as a dyed-in-the-wool anglo he wouldn't know about those things.

The producer of *Canada A.M.* tried to telephone retired Senator Eugene Forsey who knows the constitution backwards, no mean feat these days, but his cleaning lady said the Senator was writing a letter to the editor and couldn't be disturbed.

There the matter rests, with Mr. Mulroney still very much on the defensive. Staffers in the PMO, however, are saying that it's a bum rap.

DEEP END

Pat Carney

Flora MacDonald

The Shootists

The 1985 competition for the John Diefenbaker Memorial Cup for Foot Marksmanship is ancient history now, but at the time it was a real barnburner. Old Ottawa hands still go misty-eyed when they talk about it during the long winter evenings at Babylon-on-the Rideau.

First off the block, Defence Minister Robert Coates shot himself in the right foot when he thought that his inspection tour of the Canadian Forces Base at Lahr, West Germany, included a late night visit to the local sex club. How was he to know until he got the bill that the head girl's slipper held a magnum of Dom Perignon?

Then Justice Minister John Crosbie did more than justice to his left foot during a bravura performance of Newfoundland nepotism.

In the next round Fisheries Minister John Fraser winged himself in the right foot when he accepted a collect call from New Brunswick Premier Richard Hatfield with some cockamamy fish story.

Not to be upstaged, Communications Minister Marcel Masse pinked himself but good in the left foot for using his American Express Gold Card™ to treat the voters of Frontenac riding.

But when the strokes got short all contenders bowed before the Prime Minister. Old pro that he is, in one week the P.M. managed to shoot himself in *both* feet, once in Mr. Fraser's tuna tournament and again at a gala performance of the Frontenac Follies with Mr. Masse.

When Donald Fleming, Diefenbaker's old finance minister, limped onstage to present the cup, Mr. Mulroney was modest in victory. "My only regret," he told an overflow crowd at Ottawa's horse palace, "is that I have but two feet to give my country."

The Greening of the Prime Minister

Poor Pierre Trudeau! How the media clobbered him for what they saw as his presidential aspirations! They thought he wanted to make Canada into a republic with himself as President. Turns out Pierre didn't want to be President at all, just Dictator, but that's another story.

Trust Brian Mulroney to catch the idea, though, and run with it.

His role model is Ronald Reagan, another stage Irishman. To pass the time during the Shamrock Summit in Quebec City, Brian asked Ron for tips on how to be President.

"First thing, Brian me bhoy," Reagan told him, "control the cameras or they'll control you. Forget about those turkeys on Capitol Hill. The important thing is to look good on the evening news."

"I know that, Ron, but the way things have been going lately, most evenings I'd rather not be seen on the news."

The President brushed the objection aside.

"Next thing, always pick dummies for cabinet ministers. Just make sure they don't forget that you're Edgar Bergen and all they have to do is move their lips."

"No problem there, Ron. What else?"

"Stay with the Teflon look, whatever else they're showing in the fall collections. That way, if someone goofs it can't stick to you."

"But Ron, what do you do when the Teflon starts to wear thin after a while. I hear you can't repair that stuff."

"Brian, like I tell my press conferences, I've answered three questions and that is enough. Shall we join the ladies?"

Knee Jerk or Kneecap

It's not generally known, but the Father of his Country, Sir John, Eh? was really a mother.

Often tight himself, he ran his ship the same way. One of the things he would not put up with was being crossed by his ministers. "Cabinets," Sir John, Eh? used to tell Governor-General Monck, "should be kept in the closet." Which is why, early in his first term he laid down three rules that have regulated all subsequent Canajan cabinets:

1. Don't talk while the Chief is speaking.
2. Don't give the Chief an argument.
3. Don't contradict the Chief in public.

The country was reminded of these rules when the roof fell in during Mr. Mulroney's second year as P.M. and it gave Canajans a great feeling of continuity with the past.

Rules must, of course, be enforced and that means sanctions. In Sicily, the mafia practices the fine art of *omertà*, a word which freely translates as "keep your mouth shut or else." The "or else" freely translates as a kneecap job.

In Canada, Mr. Mulroney likes to play the Sicilian opening, although the threat alone is usually sufficient. For example, the Sir John, Eh? rules were applied to good effect when John Fraser, the soon-to-be-former Fisheries Minister, contradicted his Chief publicly in violation of Rule 3. Next afternoon two gentlemen from the PMO called round at the Minister's office for tea and a chat. For supper that day Mr. Fraser ate his words.

It now appears that the Sir John, Eh? rules, though originally drafted for cabinet ministers, are being applied to other ranks as well. When the Tory M.P. for Fishy Narrows, N.B., where the offending tuna-packing plant was located, disputed his Chief's

alleged lack of prior knowledge, the by-now familiar pattern emerged: a teatime visit from the PMO enforcers followed by a diet of words.

The same thing happened when the Conserve Tuv's National Director ran afoul of the Rules by contradicting his Chief's assertion that he had never heard about Communications Minister Marcel Masse's little problem with election expenses until the horsemen broke down the door. The National Director promptly disappeared without waiting for the usual invitation to tea. Press reports that he had "gone to ground" left old Ottawa hands waiting with interest for him to emerge next February 2.

Sir John, Eh? had a recipe for cabinet ministers who wouldn't stay in the closet. "If I had my way," he said, "they should all be respectable parties whom I could send to prison if I liked."

Mr. Mulroney, long an admirer of Sir John, Eh?, has not followed this recipe because of serious overcrowding in Canada's penal facilities. His ministers have, however, noted with some concern the P.M.'s announcement that a new penitentiary is to be constructed at Baie Comeau. It seems more than coincidental.

In Canada, one defies the Godfather of his Country at one's peril.

Fly Now, Pay Later through the Nose

Politicians who value their health have learned to avoid junket at all cost.

To some a harmless dessert, to others a deadly menace, it has proved a hazard to more than one politician who failed to realize its danger until too late.

The perils of junket were brought home recently to former Environment Minister Suzanne Blais-Grenier, the only Mulroney cabinet minister who wore a hyphen to work. While this lent a certain tone to meetings of caucus, it also contributed to her undoing.

Ms. Bee-Gee's trouble began when she jetted off to Paris for the weekend at Government expense. A ministerial aide had been sent ahead by plane a day earlier to inform French authorities that Ms. Blais-Grenier was one person, not two, and that, although her husband would be accompanying her, she was the minister and not he.

The French, unaccustomed to the finer points of Canajan usage, failed to understand this and prepared lunch for a large party. Officials were miffed when only the minister and her husband showed up after the Quai d'Orsay had sent out for pizza for three. To give credit where it is due, a quick-thinking Ms. Blais-Grenier saved the day by asking the French *sous-ministre* (who was wearing a hyphen for the occasion) if she could have a doggie bag.

From there on, though, it was downhill all the way. According to her press officer, Ms. Blais-Grenier had gone to Paris to pick up on her ecology. Critics, however, alerted by media reports that she had been seen checking price-tags at Givenchy, were quick to point out that Canada had too much ecology already and, given present high levels of unemployment, should not be bringing in more of it, particularly when produced by cheap foreign labor.

At that point someone in the House uttered the word "junket" and with that the polyunsaturated was in the fire for sure. In vain did Ms. Blais-Grenier's press secretary insist that his minister had personally paid all travel costs not incurred on Government business and had the receipts to prove it. When challenged to produce the receipts he confessed that they were somewhere in the minister's purse which she hadn't got to the bottom of yet.

The aide insisted that Ms. Blais-Grenier had attended only official functions in Paris. When challenged with a press report that his minister had been overheard saying to the doorman at the Ritz: "Garçon, où est le Louvre?" he insisted that in fact she had been asking for the loo, not the Louvre, and had gone there on official business.

The Prime Minister, impressed by her ability to stretch a weekend in Paris to include side-trips to Stockholm, Corsica, Helsinki and Leningrad, removed Ms. Blais-Grenier from the sensitive Environment portfolio and appointed her Minister of State for Transport.

Although the P.M. had hoped she would be a shot in the arm for the railways, it turned out Ms. Blais-Grenier suffers from travel sickness. She got off at the first stop leaving her new portfolio behind.

A New Right?

Ours is a negative age and the Conserve Tuvs, as always, are at the blunt edge of change.

It is an age of disinformation, of deflation, of disincentives, of reverse heels on shoes, of defoliation, of detoxification. Add to them the right not to know. Wisely used it has saved many a politician from disaster.

Although Mr. Mulroney has invoked the right more often than any prime minister in this century, contrary to popular belief he did not invent it.

How did it all begin? Picture a winter evening in the year 1916. The month is February, the day the 3rd, the time 8:47 p.m. Sir Robert Borden, Canada's wartime Prime Minister is sitting in his study sipping a hot toddy and playing two-handed whist with his butler when the door bursts open and a breathless aide rushes in.

"Sir, sir, the Parliament Buildings are on fire!"

"Please don't tell me about it, Jenkins."

"But sir, they're burning down! All your papers will be lost, your books, your income tax returns, your— "

"I told you, I don't want to hear about it."

"But why, sir, why?"

"So that if I'm asked in Question Period I can honestly say that the first time I heard about it was on the CBC evening news."

"But— but sir, the CBC won't be established until 1936."

"And *that's* when I want to hear about it."

Later prime ministers often invoked the right not to know, although none more creatively than Brian Mulroney, whose ignorance on politically embarrassing subjects never fails to impress observers. To his credit, though, no sooner does he hear about a problem than he moves speedily to set things to rights.

Item: the tainted tuna caper. "Never heard a word, but the minute I got wind of it (choke!) I bloody well took the stuff off the shelves. Even the cat wouldn't eat it. We're sending it to Ethiopia."

Item: Suzanne Blais-Grenier's holiday junket to Europe at government expense. "It's news to me, but as soon as I heard we straightened things out. You know how women are about keeping track of their expenses. Why, I have to help Mila balance her checkbook every month."

Item: the R.C.M.P. investigation of Marcel Masse's election expenses. "No one told me a thing, s'help me. When I found out of course I accepted his resignation at once, it's the least I could do for the poor bugger."

The right not to know has proved so useful politically that the provincial premiers want Ottawa to make it available on a regional basis. At last reports Richard Hatfield of New Brunswick was calling for a constitutional amendment to include it in the Charter of Rights and Freedoms.

You've had a Dose of your own Madison, Avenue?

Those who live by the evening news shall die by the evening news.

Such is the First Rule of Canajan politics and the Prime Minister is learning this the hard way.

For the first twelve months of his reign, Mr. Mulroney held the media in the palm of his hand. Not since a man with a rose turned Canajans into a nation of maniacs had a political leader enjoyed such unchallenged media control. As his own producer, director and male lead, Mr. Mulroney appeared in a series of TV specials that left his public enchanted and the critics speechless. With every performance, whether major part or cameo role, his ratings went up. When he and President Reagan did a soft-shoe number with vocals at the Shamrock Summit stardom beckoned: an Emmy, a Grammy, even— who knows?— an Oscar seemed within his grasp.

Like Pavarotti or Dolly Parton there was no end to Mr. Mulroney's rise in the ratings. As for his political rivals, to judge by the trifling amount of media coverage they received, John Turner and Ed Broadbent might just as well have been playing a kazoo duet in an Aklavik honky-tonk.

Then, overnight, the P.M.'s life changed from media event to sitcom. Gone were the unquestioning adulation, the uncritical acclaim, the roll-over-and-play-dead media treatment. Gone too was much of the Music Man's self-assurance that had sustained them.

Suddenly the star was dodging cabbages. A string of cabinet ministers started getting the hook and the dialogue fell to the level of: "I didn't"— "You did!" "You're a liar!"— "You're another!" For the first time ever, the P.M.'s ratings tumbled.

A recent poll conducted by the Canajan Press among residents of the little mountain village of Credibility Gap, B.C., disclosed that 67.3 per cent would not buy a used car from Mr. Mulroney.

The Sound of Chin Music

A new epidemic has struck Parliament Hill.

The Prime Minister, having seen his band more or less safely through a series of political afflictions including a fish allergy, galloping nepotism, endemic electoral hanky-panky, foot-in-the-mouth disease and bankrupture, now finds himself confronting a new threat to the health of his administration.

The latest outbreak has been tentatively diagnosed as *logorrhea politicalis*. This is a disabling, although rarely fatal, affliction that occurs among legislators of every stripe. We know it by the more familiar name of verbal diarrhea or "politician's disease."

So far, medical researchers have charted three stages of the condition:

1. Common logorrhea (*l. vulgaris*), a low-level infection that attacks all politicians early in life. Treatment: two aspirins every four hours and get lots of rest.

2. Infectious logorrhea (*l. virulens*), also known as verbal herpes. The victim is now a danger to the community. Avoid intercourse. Treatment: isolate the patient.

3. Advanced or chronic logorrhea. No known treatment, although muscle relaxants may be taken to ease lingual cramp. Prognosis: incurable.

John Crosbie, himself a victim of the third or terminal stage of the disease, has spelled out some of its dangers. Speaking recently on an open-line show at St. John's, the Terror of the Outports said it all with his usual brevity. "The Conservatives talk too much," he told a caller, "when it is quite unnecessary to be talking. As a result of talking too much, they get contradictions." Prime Minister

Mulroney is known to be looking at various remedies for this social disease which has struck down so many from his own party. The PMO is showing interest in a lip button being developed by the National Research Council, but clinical testing has yet to begin and Health and Welfare approval is a long way off.

Meantime, the latest outbreak has epidemiologists worried.

Come on in, the Water's Hot

Fitness Minister Otto Jelinek has joined the list of cabinet ministers who are in *agua caliente.*

For a time it looked as though only senior ministers could qualify for immersion—Finance, Defence, Justice, Fisheries, Communications, Industry—but the finger of fate does not play favorites.

First Mr. Jelinek, citing a death in the family, cancelled a meeting with workers facing layoffs in his riding. Then, on the same day, he was snapped by a press photographer attending a Blue Jays game with his leader, Mr. Mulroney.

Mr. Jelinek should have known better.

Even the office boy could have told him that only in the comic strips do people get to the ball game by telling the boss that they have to go to their grandmother's funeral.

Welcome to the hot tub club, Otto, but next time speak to the office boy first.

Patronage Is My Age, Pat; How Old Are You?

When Brian Mulroney was hitting the campaign trail during the last federal election, you would have thought he hadn't a friend in the world.

You could tell that from the way he wrinkled his nose at John Turner's attempts to justify patronage during the television debates. He called it vulgar when the departing Prime Minister handed out sweetheart appointments to seventeen retiring M.P.s on the very day he announced the federal election. Stressing that a clean-living guy from Baie Comeau could never be guilty of such impure conduct, Mr. Mulroney called it "the boys cutting up the cash."

Well, Came the Dawn, as they used to say in the silent movies. Once firmly in the saddle, the new P.M. began distributing political largesse with all the restraint of a runaway manure spreader. Suddenly it seemed he had nothing *but* friends and all of them were getting sweetheart appointments. School chums. Business chums. Law chums. Political chums. Chums of chums. The appointments came so fast and furious that the big Order-in-Council machine in the PMO burned out and had to be replaced with a heavy-duty model. Before you could say Svend Robinson, every political appointment in the country had flipped over like a flapjack. Overnight, Liberals were out, Conserve Tuvs were in. The CBC. Air Canada. CN. The Bank of Canada. The Baie Comeau Committee for the 1988 Olympics. You name it. Everywhere you looked, it was wall-to-wall friends. Mr. Mulroney had promised a policy of national reconciliation and that's what he delivered. Never before had Canada been such a friendly place.

When challenged over this orgy of patronage, Mr. Mulroney waxed indignant.

"Only appointing friends? Who, me? Say, just go find me an enemy and watch me appoint him to something."

It proved to be a safe challenge. The media hunted high. The media hunted low. Search though they might, not an enemy could be found. True enough, someone did discover an Enemies of Brian Mulroney Club in Baie Comeau, of all places, but it was no go. Turned out to have only two members, both of them relatives of the P.M.

"Oh-h, I couldn't appoint *them,*" the Prime Minister told a press conference, "They're pixillated. Besides, that would be nepotism. What do you think this is, Newfoundland?"

Then someone in the PMO thought of two gadflies who were always buzzing around Conserve Tuv flanks—Stephen Lewis gadding about Ontario and Dennis McDermott flying all over the place. How to get rid of them? Nothing to it. A light sprinkling with the holy water of patronage and—hey, presto!—in place of two mortal enemies of Brian Mulroney there stood two bosom friends clutching airline tickets (one-way) to New York and Dublin, with not a buzz to be heard from either of them. It was sheer magic.

Everyone knows what Mr. Mulroney promised the Canajan people if they elected him—jobs, jobs, jobs. And what did they get? Jobs, jobs, jobs— for friends of Brian Mulroney.

Whatever else, you can't say that the Prime Minister is not a man of his word.

Fiscal Culture

Canajans need toughening up. That's the latest word from the Economic Council of Canada (ECCH).

ECCH reported that twenty years of easy living under the Liberals left us fiscally soft. Out of condition. Flabby. It seems that when Mr. Mulroney and his Conserve Tuvs took us in hand we had already lost most of our energy, despite a national energy policy; our balance of payments was way off balance; our tax loopholes had holes in them; and our national product was gross. After Mr. Mulroney had looked at the books, he confirmed the ECCH'S worst fears. The country was in an advanced state of bankrupture or financial hernia.

This should have surprised nobody. The Liberals, following strict Keynesian dogma, had for years been throwing money at every problem in sight. On days when there were no problems they threw money anyway. Force of habit. One year they even tried to organize a money-throwing competition at the Highland Games, of all places, that's how remote from reality the Grits had grown. No wonder Canada became the first Western nation to make the trip to the poorhouse in a Mercedes.

When Mr. Mulroney took over he told Canajans that, contrary to popular belief, he was not a son of any dogma. He also announced that the days of Liberal free spending were over. *Fini*, in the bilingual version. He told Canajans that tough times called for tough measures. Belts would be tightened. Costs would be cut. Free-loaders would be off-loaded. A regime of fiscal exercise and cold showers would produce a leaner, cleaner nation. Tough love would be the order of the day. Critics called it an over-ambitious program, but accountants whose most strenuous form of exercise for years had been lifting copies of the Income Tax Act nodded their heads sagely in agreement.

First came the cuts. To show that he meant business Mr. Mulroney cut every Liberal appointee off the public payroll, starting with his old friend Bryce Mackasey. No room for friendship, now. Sorry, Bryce, but that's how things are. Best of luck, though. Cost-cutting became the order of the day as one Liberal after another got the chop. The board of Canada Post: chop. The board of Via Rail: chop. The board of Canadair: chop. The board of the National Arts Centre: chop. The board of Petro-Canada: chop. The board of Eldorado Nuclear: chop.

Overnight, Mr. Mulroney and his little chopper had trimmed millions of dollars worth of fat from the body politic. Everyone could see the difference. And with all that money saved, taxpayers across the nation heaved a collective sigh of relief. People felt better at seeing Liberal waste eliminated. For the first time in living memory the Auditor-General went around whistling while he worked. A new era lay ahead.

And then a funny thing happened on the way to the new era. As fast as they had been chopped all those boards of directors sprang up again, only now instead of being composed exclusively of bad Liberals they were staffed with nothing but good Conserve Tuvs. It made all the difference.

A few cynics went around muttering, but Mr. Mulroney pointed out that he hadn't promised them a rose garden. In trying times like these, he told a desk-thumping House of Commons, all he had to offer Canajans was tough talk, tough love and tough titty.

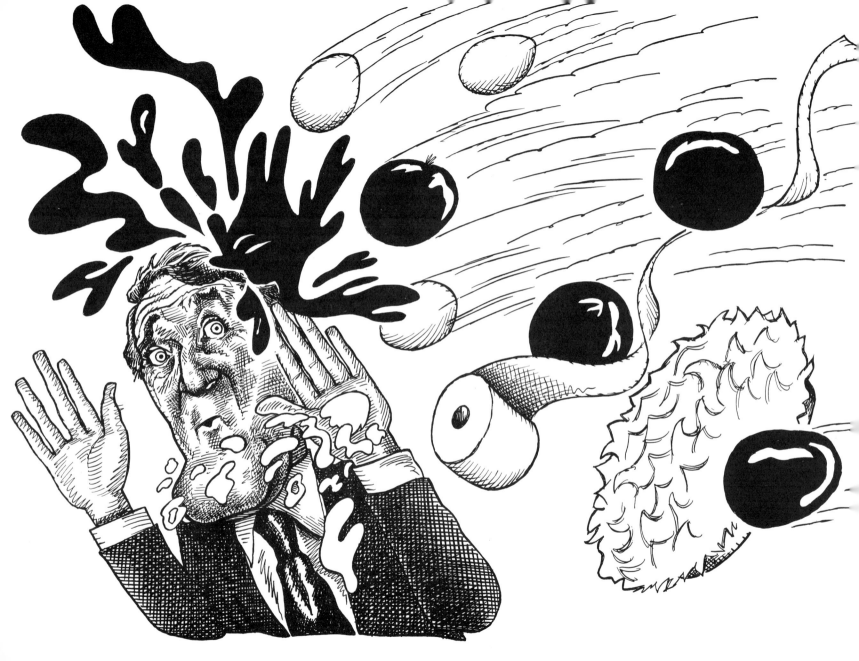

Mulroney's Law

The Prime Minister has discovered a new law. By common agreement it will bear Mr. Mulroney's name in the same way that plants are often called after the botanist who first discovered them.

The P.M. found out about Mulroney's Law the hard way. It took time but isn't that how all great laws get discovered? Don't ever think that Sir Isaac Newton discovered the law of gravity the first time an apple hit him on the head. No way. He just kept sitting under the tree and it wasn't until several bushels of pippins had bounced off his noggin that he got the message. A lesser man would have moved away from the tree sooner, but not Newton. He knew that there had to be a reason why he kept getting hit on the head and he was right. It just took time to figure out.

Mr. Mulroney had to go through much the same process in order to discover his law. The House of Commons was his apple tree. Whenever he sat there something was sure to hit him on the head, particularly during Question Period. The air would be full of flying objects some of which were sure to land on his head, dodge though he might. It got so he positively disliked sitting in the House. Parliament, which had been the breath of life to his illustrious predecessor, John Diefenbaker, who delighted in returning blow for blow, was fast becoming the kiss of death for him.

Then the P.M. made a startling discovery. One day he was called away from the House of Commons on important business at the beginning of Question Period. When he returned some hours later he noticed that then House Leader Erik Nielsen was holding his head. He looked groggy. That evening over dinner as 24 Sussex Drive the P.M. sat lost in thought, toying with his shepherd's pie.

"A hard day at the office, Brian?"

"Uh-huh. They're all about the same, Mila."

"How's the head?"

"Well, it's a funny thing but it doesn't seem to be bothering me as much tonight. I can't figure it out."

"Maybe you're just getting used to the House of Commons?"

"Me? Never. That bloody Opposition never gives me any respect."

"Poor dear! So what was different about today?"

"I dunno. Wait, I wasn't there for Question Period and nothing hit me on the head. Say, maybe I'm on to something! Yeah, yeah, if I skip Question Period tomorrow, they won't have me to kick around any more. Let me think . . ."

Well, as they say, the rest is history. Starting with Question Period the P.M. absented himself from the House for more and more time each day and— lo and behold!— he wasn't getting hit on the head any longer. Whatever the issue— Tunagate, Blais-Grenier's expense account, banks going belly up, patronage, you name it— someone else's head got all the lumps.

That's when they enacted Mulroney's Law which states: "If you ain't there, they can't hit you on the head." It was the greatest thing since Ronald Reagan discovered Teflon.

Old Ottawa hands have been quick to point out that Mulroney's Law is not new, being in fact a restatement of Murphy's Law ("If it ain't broke, don't fix it"), but the PMO insists that it's a first.

What's Better in the Bahamas?

Once again the Prime Minister has broken with tradition.

Most Canajans jet off to the Bahamas to get away from the cold. Mr. Mulroney went to Nassau to get away from the heat. After the firestorm he had been through on Parliament Hill the burning sun of New Providence came as blessed relief.

The trip also gave him a chance to be on camera with the big names among the Commonwealth heads of state.

The second morning, Prime Minister Robert Mugabe of Zimbabwe was having a session with press photographers when the P.M. edged up to his party.

"Hi Bob! I'm Brian, remember me?"

"Mmm."

"A grand morning, isn't it?"

"Mmm."

"You know, only last night I was telling Mila, she's the wife, y'know, all about your great country."

"Mmm."

"Wait till I take my glasses off, fellows. Yeah, like I was saying, when I was a '*tit gars* in Baie Comeau, that's in Kuhbek, y'know, I had this collection of stamps and some of the African issues were just super."

"Mmm."

"Well, thanks, fellows. O.K., Bob, have a nice day."

"Mmm."

But Nassau wasn't all fun and games. First the duty calls: tea with the Queen, pretty good for a truck driver from Baie Comeau, eh? Then a visit to the local laundromat to check out press reports that branches of Canajan banks had been laundering drug money. Couldn't find anything but a soapy floor.

The big argument was about sanctions against South Africa which gave the P.M. his chance to play the Big Reconciler. All week he slaved over a hot agenda and finally succeeded in knocking the smallest microchip of rust off the Iron Lady. The P.M. exulted that he had made the lady move enormously in the direction of sanctions, a claim somewhat flawed by Mrs. Thatcher's boast that she had compromised only a tiny little bit. At the closing press conference the African first ministers had nothing but praise for the P.M.'s achievement.

"Mr. Mugabe, did Prime Minister Mulroney make Mrs. Thatcher move enormously or only a tiny little bit?"

"Mmm."

HEADS UP, YOU MEDIA PEOPLE, I'M OVER HERE . . .

The Woman Thou Gavest Me

A new day has dawned for Canajan women.

Beginning with Marie Hébert who pulled the plough for her husband Louis, the first farmer of New France, Canajan women have struggled slowly and painfully towards the light.

Three hundred years after Marie Hébert won the country's first ploughing match the Supreme Court of Canada solemnly decided in 1928 that women were non-persons, not fit to be senators. Well, the Privy Council quickly squashed *that* notion on appeal, deciding that women were indeed fit to be senators, which isn't saying a lot about women when you come to think of it. In any case, that decision didn't end the matter because almost sixty years later another clutch of judges in another case decided just as solemnly that girls couldn't play on a boys' hockey team. Must be because girls aren't persons or something, which just goes to show that you can't teach an old judge new tricks.

Well, the Conserve Tuvs have changed all that. They elected more women to Parliament than any political party in history; they appointed more women as cabinet ministers than any political party in history; and they have given more responsibility to women cabinet ministers than any political party in history.

Take former Minister of State for Finance Barbara McDougall, for example, who had single-handedly been holding the fort for the Government on the big bank scandal. For the first time in more than sixty years not one but two Canajan banks bit the dust and who got the job of handling this delicate operation? Not men, for sure. When it came to facing the House and the nation there wasn't a man to be found. The P.M. was like elsewhere, Finance Minister Michael Wilson had laryngitis and Bank of Canada Governor Bouey's lips were sealed because everybody knows that bankers never cry. The rest of the cabinet was out to lunch as usual.

It was Barbara McDougall who faced the nation with a bold front. A lot of people wondered why she looked so edgy giving us the bad news on camera; after all, it wasn't her money that was going down the tubes. *Now* it turns out that she was against the bailout from the start. When a bunch of the fellows brought it up in caucus she said absolutely not. No way. But although she put her No. 9D down firmly, the guys ganged up on her and decided to go for the bundle regardless when the P.M. told them he wasn't going to have any bank failures during *his* term of office and that was that.

Well, Barbara went along like a good kid; what else could she do? But her heart wasn't in it. Of course just because she delivered the message everybody jumped to the conclusion that the billion-dollar bailout was *her* idea and proceeded to dump on her. One sob-sister even called her "the elegant widow who closes banks." With women like that, who needs men?

At that point did the Prime Minister say that the bailout was his idea and not hers? He did not. Did Finance Minister Michael Wilson say it was his idea and not hers? Are you kidding? Did Bank of Canada President Gerald Bouey say it was his idea and not hers? What a hope! Did— well, you get the general idea.

Mind you, that required a lot of brave talk from Barbara, most of it defensive, ranging from "I don't apologize for trying to save the banks" to "The bank failures give me no problem in my soul." That soul talk wasn't bad for an elegant widow.

So don't ever accuse the Conserve Tuvs of not giving women the big jobs. Look at good old Barbara! When the chips were down she got to carry the can all by herself.

Backward, Turn Backward O Time, in Your Flight

There are days when we wish we could go back to bed and start over again.

It can't be done, though. Whether we like it or not, life can only be lived in one direction: forward.

Champions know this. When Luis Firpo knocked Jack Dempsey clear out of the ring in the first round of their heavyweight title bout, did Dempsey ask the referee if he could go back to bed and then start the fight over again? He did not. The Manassa Mauler just climbed back into the ring and proceeded to knock Firpo all the way to Buenos Aires in the second round. That's what they call the right stuff nowadays.

Mr. Mulroney seems to have forgotten about the Dempsey-Firpo match. After being knocked out of the ring by an Opposition one-third his size the P.M. feels that if he went back to bed and started over again things would be better. He thinks that if he stayed out of the ring for a while people would forget what happened in the first round.

Sorry, Brian, but that's not how Jack Dempsey would have done it.

Sovereign Tea

The Canajan North is all things to all people. Home of Inuit and iceworms. Virgin expanse awaiting the polluter's hand. Place where Sam McGee was cremated. Biggest ice cube in the *Guiness Book of Records*.

Trouble is, it's not Canajan according to the Americans. They say only the solid parts belong to Canada; the liquid parts in between the solid parts are international. That's international for Americans you understand, not international for Russians. Makes all the difference.

External Affairs told the U.S. that the liquid parts are solid in winter and so by definition belong to Canada, at least while they're solid. But the Americans sent back a note saying if we can ram an icebreaker through, then solid is the same as liquid and so's your old man.

Our friends are saying it's a funny kind of iced sovereign tea, though, solid in winter and liquid in summer. Only in Canada for sure.

The whole business really is a puzzler with no precedents to guide us. External has asked Israel to send along a copy of the legal opinion obtained by Moses when the Lord divided the waters of the Red Sea to let the Exodus crowd through. They figure it could have a bearing.

Meantime, the P.M. is thinking of sending Joe Clark up north to establish a Canajan presence. That should kill two birds with one stone.

Nuthin' fer Nuthin'

The best things in life are free, they used to tell us. Free lunch. Free air. Free love.

Add to them free trade.

The Mulroney Conserve Tuvs, who have botched everything they set their hand to, are now trying to convince us that free trade with the United States will solve all our woes. Also theirs.

Could be. Having failed to deliver on their promise of all the foreign capital that was supposed to arrive the day after they took over, not to mention jobs, jobs, jobs, the Conserve Tuvs badly need to boost their ratings.

Trouble is, if we go with free trade we're bucking a trend. Anything free is passé lately. Free lunch? Went out in grandpa's day along with the nickel glass of beer. Free air? Most gas stations are charging for it these days. Don't offer to clean your windshield, either. Free love? We know what that led to, don't we?

So what can we expect from free trade with the U.S. once the protective membrane of tariffs is removed— mercantile herpes?

Taking the Grunt Out of Immigrunt

Canada was built on the backs of her sons and daughters. The strong backs, that is. You can't be hewers of wood and drawers of water with a bad back. Just ask any chiropractor.

Most young nations— Canada, the U.S.A., Australia— were built on backs. Strong backs. Wetbacks. Outbacks. Add to them greenbacks.

That's the latest message to the downtrodden of the world from the Mulroney Conserve Tuvs who are on the lookout for moneyed immigrants. Any downtrodden of the world with a quarter of a million bucks to invest are more than welcome. That's a big change from the old days when the inscription on the Statue of Liberty ran: "Give me your tired, your poor, your huddled masses..." Now word has gone out to the tired and the poor: If you've got $250,000 just step right up for your visas. And to the huddled masses the password is C.O.D.

Seems like Canada doesn't need strong backs any more. Chinese labor built the transcontinental railways— but the transcontinental trains don't run any more. Farm workers from half-a-dozen European countries held the plough that broke the plains that grew the wheat. Now the farmers are broke along with the plains. West Indian labor picked the tobacco crop— but tobacco is a drug on the market these days, you should pardon the expression, since we started putting fine print on the cigarette package.

Oh, a few Anglo-Saxon and Asian immigrunts will still be needed to do the traditional jobs: Hugh will hew the wood and Hue will draw the water. For the rest, though, our immigration policy will be based on color. And the color is green.

NO ENTRY

Run Spot, Run, Watch how the Watch-Dog Dogs

We have too many generals in Ottawa and not enough privates.

That's the latest word from the Auditor-General and he should know.

The Auditor-General's closet has traditionally housed more skeletons than Dr. Frankenstein's waiting-room. Over the years he has chilled our blood with more horror stories than Bela Lugosi.

Critics used to blame this state of affairs on twenty years of Liberal misrule and the Conserve Tuvs were glad to join in the hue and cry. Now, however, it's the Mulroney Conserve Tuvs who are getting the hueing and crying and they don't like it. Unfortunately, they have no one else to blame.

One example will suffice to give the flavor of the Mulroney years. It seems that several Crown corporations located in Ottawa who routinely borrow hundreds of millions from the Feds have made a lot of moola by sending their loan repayments across town to the Feds by regular post. That way when someone duns them they can say with a perfectly straight face: "The cheque is in the mail." Meantime they save themselves a bundle in unpaid interest when their cheques take two weeks to go across Ottawa via Nanaimo. Crown corporations certainly weren't that smart in Liberal days, but then no one was interested in saving money in those days either.

Former Industry Minister Sinclair Stevens, for one, can't see what the Auditor-General is making such a fuss about. Speaking to reporters as he dropped his rent cheque in the parliamentary mail-box, he said: "It's just a matter of creative financing. In the private sector we call it leverage."

No More Killing Fields

No one can say that Canada is not doing her bit to ease international tensions.

A recent news item reported that the Canajan Forces are purchasing a hundred million dollars worth of M-16 rifles from the United States at a time when the U.S. Army is phasing out the M-16 in favor of a more advanced weapon.

The effectivenesss of the M-16 has been called in question because the rifle jammed frequently when used by American troops in Vietnam.

Our government is to be congratulated. By equipping her armed forces with rifles that do not shoot, Canada has struck a significant blow for world peace.

The Wall is Getting Stonier

It's harder than hard to find someone to accept blame for the great banking scandal.

First they tried to lay it at the P.M.'s door.

"Mr. Mulroney," a reporter asked at the back door of 24 Sussex Drive, "are you to blame for the great banking scandal?"

"As God is my judge, I didn't know a thing about it until I heard Barbara on *The Journal*."

"Barbara McDougall?"

"No, Barbara Frum."

Next the reporter called on the Minister of Finance.

"Mr. Wilson, are you to blame for the great banking scandal?"

"Sorry, I've been out of town. You'll have to ask Barbara about that."

"Barbara Frum?"

"No, Barbara McDougall."

The reporter cornered the then Minister of State for Finance, a.k.a. the Widow Who Closes Banks, after Question Period.

"Mrs. McDougall, are you to blame for the great banking scandal?"

"I have nothing to add to my statement in the House."

The next stop on the line was the Bank of Canada.

"Mr. Bouey, are you to blame for the great banking scandal?"

"The important thing is not to point your finger at the most powerful banker in the country," Mr. Bouey answered reproachfully, "but to find out what went wrong."

"So who *do* we point the finger at?"

"I think you mean 'whom.' I was relying on the bank examiner's report. You'll have to finger somebody else."

And so it goes. Next thing, they'll be blaming one of the cleaning ladies in the office of the Inspector-General of Banks. Nobody wants to be the guy who falls.

This unseemly merry-go-round must stop if confidence in the banking system is to be restored. It's crystal clear that the people to blame for the great banking scandal are the ones who insisted on depositing their money in the failing banks after the government assured them that it was perfectly safe to do so.

Let's lay blame where blame is due.

Everything but the Kitchen Sink

An army, Napoleon used to tell Josephine when he was late getting home, travels on its stomach. In those days it made for slow progress, but at least it didn't cost much. Not any more, though. This lesson was brought home by a recent announcement that the government approved spending $585,341 on a new kitchen for the Governor-General's residence. The price tag led some observers to wonder who is the chatelaine at Rideau Hall anyway, Madame Sauvé or Madame Benoit.

The kitchen in question is said to measure 372 square metres. By reporting its size in metric the government has managed once again to pull the oilcloth over our eyes. They first did this with gasoline prices when they switched the pumps from gallons to litres. Motorists were encouraged to believe that a litre was something like a gallon, only more continental. The change made them feel as though they were driving a BMW instead of a Chevy, so they never stopped to think what the price of gas worked out to in gallons.

Now they're giving us the size of Madame Sauvé's kitchen in square metres, for heaven's sake, so no one can figure out whether we're getting a good deal for our $585,341. And this is after the Conserve Tuvs told us we could use imperial *or* metric, no sweat. Evidently they think that's fine when it comes to a pound of hamburger at the supermarket, but not so fine when it comes to Madame Sauvé's kitchen.

One thing is clear: at today's prices, travelling on your stomach ain't cheap.

Contact Sports in Parliament

Environment Minister Thomas McMillan was quick to join the defenders of his predecessor, Suzanne Blais-Grenier, whose travel costs on her junkets to Europe staggered even American Express.

Earlier, then Deputy Prime Minister Erik Nielsen had accused Opposition critics of racism when they demanded to see her receipts, only to back down grudgingly under Opposition pressure for an apology.

It now turns out that Ms. Blais-Grenier blew $46,947.39 for a couple of trips to Europe where most of her time was spent on private holidays with her husband whom she married when she didn't have a hyphen to her name. One of the items was $4,000 for a chauffeur-driven limo that took the young couple from Paris to Brittany and back. Turns out they didn't realize that meters on Paris taxis drop $5 every quarter-mile as anyone who was ever taken for a ride by a French taxi-driver could have told them.

Now Mr. McMillan has come forward with a new defence of his embattled colleague. "I think," he told reporters outside the House, "to some extent she's been given a bum rap."

His remark struck a memory chord among Ottawa watchers who recalled how Opposition Leader John Turner fell from grace during the last election campaign when he tried the same manoeuvre on Iona Campagnolo.

Honorable members should bear in mind that there are more dangerous things in politics than racism.

Making Water

Way back in the good old days, Pierre Trudeau, the last Canajan prime minister who could read and write, used to say that being a neighbor of the United States was like sleeping with an elephant.

Everything was great until the elephant decided to roll over in bed.

Trouble was, Pierre didn't carry the simile far enough. The *really* big problem is what to do when the elephant decides to use the bed for a litter pan.

That's no small matter as anyone who has ever followed behind an elephant can attest. And the Americans, having thoroughly fouled their own environment along with a good deal of ours, are now looking for new worlds to pollute. Northward the course of Empire takes its way, as the feller might have said.

Mr. Mulroney brings this to mind with his choice of Simon Reisman as Canada's ambassador to the U.S. free-trade talks. All hands agree that Mr. Reisman is the ideal fox to guard the Canajan hen-roost. A former deputy minister of finance turned private consultant in Ottawa, he had been acting for a group that plans to turn James Bay into a freshwater lake and ship the water south to the U.S. through a $100-billion network of canals, dams and tunnels. Since the U.S. wants water so badly, Simon says, it could be our best bargaining card to gain access for Canajan goods to the U.S. market.

Methinks yon Reisman doth go too far, as another feller might have said. Besides, his idea is just plain bad merchandising. If we sell off our clean H_2O first, who will buy the dirty stuff that's left? Far better to keep our good James Bay water on ice, as it were, and unload the foul and filthy fluid first on the unsuspecting Yankees.

We might start with the St. Clair River, a stream of effluent flowing between Lakes Urine and Eerie that American industry has

77

been using as a toilet bowl for generations. Mr. Reisman should talk his clients into buying that water first. It may take a bit of selling, but with the help of the Master Salesman from Baie Comeau Mr. Reisman should be able to pull it off. Next they might unload the downstream water from the Love Canal which has been discharging so much toxic waste into the system that it made the Niagara Gorge rise.

In fact, a draft or two from the St. Clair River followed by a moonlight sail on the Love Canal could slake America's thirst for Canajan water permanently.

You Can't Teach an Old Dog New Metrics

Once again Canajans have fallen victim to government metrickery.

It was a previous Liberal administration that dragged Canada kicking and screaming into the Eighteenth Century by forcibly replacing the Imperial way of measurement with the metric system.

The metric system was first foisted, or possibly foist firsted, on an unsuspecting world by the French Revolutionaries. Firstly, or foistly, they abolished the monarchy by separating Louis the Sixteenth from his crown without bothering to remove it from his head. Then they brought in the metric system, thereby so confusing the common people that they couldn't even take the measure of the Terror which had been unleashed in the name of Liberty, let alone the weight of a fistful of sausages at the local *charcuterie*. When they finally figured out what had happened it was too late to do anything except grouse about it. That has been the public's reaction to metricization ever since.

In our troubled day Canajan governments saw metric as a way out. During the Seventies things had begun to come loose. People were fed up with everything measurable. The temperature was too low in winter. Lakes and rivers were too high in the spring. The weather was too hot in summer. In fall the barometer read 29.7 inches and falling. Prices were too high all year round and public approval was at an all-time low. While the government tried hard, all the voters ever did was bitch, bitch, bitch.

That's when the Liberals took their giant step backwards. Remembering how France had confounded the populace and ended discontent during the French Revolution by changing the measurements of everything, they proceeded to do the same thing.

It was a stroke of pure genius. Overnight, people forgot about inflation, unemployment, the international situation, cellulite, you

79

name it, because they were so busy trying to figure out the size, weight and cost of things. Who could grumble if the barometric pressure measured 1003 kilopascals and falling? With that big a number they still had a long way to go before hitting bottom, so why worry?

Well sir, just when things had reached the stage of advanced frustration along came then Consumer Minister Michel Côté with a huge mandate to clean up the whole mess. When in Opposition, the Conserve Tuvs had pounded, or rather kilogrammed, the Liberals over metric. Now was their big chance to right the great Canajan wrong.

So what happened? Well, as usual, they flubbed it. After much deliberation Mr. Côté unveiled his master plan: metric would remain the law of the land but his ministry would not enforce it by prosecuting Imperialists. In other words, metric was still official, but not officially official.

It sounded all too familiar.

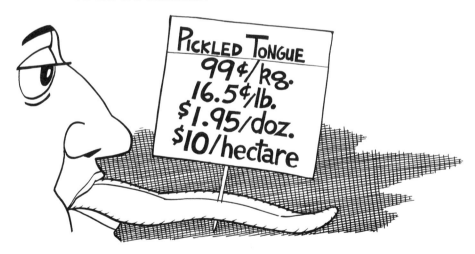

The Invisible Man

Mulroney's Law has finally caught on. That's the latest word from Babylon-on-the-Rideau where the PMO has briefed every last Conserve Tuv on the law.

Mulroney's Law, it will be remembered, decrees that if you ain't there they can't hit you on the head.

As a result, not since the days of Mackenzie King ("government if necessary, but not necessarily government"), has any administration achieved such a low profile. Thanks to a strict application of the new law, on most days no one seems to be in charge on Parliament Hill.

This was demonstrated during a recent CBC television survey.

"Excuse me, sir, could you tell me who's in charge on Parliament Hill?"

"Uh, Joe Clark?"

"Excuse me, madam— "

"Don't call *me* madam!"

"Excuse me, Ms. Can you tell me who's in charge on Parliament Hill?"

"Pierre Juneau."

"Excuse me, sir. Can you tell me who's in charge on Parliament Hill?"

"Uh, John uh..."

The disappearance of every single member of the Mulroney administration, including the P.M. himself, left the media without a victim. For the first week or so the newscasters got by with stock shots: Mr. Mulroney sneaking a quick puff in the parliamentary washroom; former Defence Minister Robert Coates buying another round of drinks at the Kitchie-Koo Club in Lahr, West Germany; former Fisheries Minister John Fraser with tuna on his face; former Environment Minister Suzanne Blais-Grenier riding on a camel; former Justice Minister John Crosbie with his mouth open.

But as days went by the truth finally began to dawn on Canajans: the government had vanished.

Some cabinet ministers disappeared better than others, none more completely that George Hees, the doughty Veterans' Affairs Minister. It seems that at the time of his swearing-in ceremony Mr. Hees also swore allegiance to Mulroney's Law. By never saying anything either in the House or elsewhere he contradicted nobody, nor could he be contradicted. By practicing the art of invisibility he survived the epidemic of scandals and resignations that decimated the Conserve Tuv cabinet. So well did he adhere to the Law that most people thought he had died years ago and were surprised when he appeared on television last Remembrance Day.

Old Ottawa hands have been quick to say it's not Mulroney's Law that made Mr. Hees invisible so much as the lesson learned as a member of John Diefenbaker's cabinet. Amid the scandals that rocked the final days of the Diefenbaker regime, Mr. Hees gained instant notoriety as The Man Who Took Gerda Munsinger to Lunch. For the longest while it looked as though his career had reached Endsville.

Well sir, old soldier that he is, George Hees fought his way back to respectability. He forsook his former haunts. He worked selflessly among the poor and outcast. He gave up eating lunch and yes, he followed Mulroney's Law to the letter.

The result? Today he sits on the Government benches serene and invisible, his silvery head intact while all about him are losing theirs and blaming it on effete media snobs.

So why go on being invisible? Come out from behind the door, George; the Gerda Munsinger affair is completely forgotten.

Giving Away the Store

People used to wonder what would happen when kids who watched thirty hours of television a week grew up.

Now we know. They became Mulroney Conserve Tuvs.

Everyone has heard about the Prime Minister's addiction to television, but few people realize how strongly the attitudes of Mr. Mulroney and his cabinet ministers were molded by what they saw on the little screen during their formative years. It explains their stand on public issues.

Like Question Period. Remember *Front Page Challenge?*

Like the health care field. Remember *M*A*S*H*?*

Like the P.M.'s crisis management strategy. Remember *This Was the Week that Was?*

Like freedom of information. Remember *I've Got a Secret?*

But most of all they were conditioned by the giveaway shows of the Sixties and Seventies. Those were the programs that used to hand out a warehouse full of goodies to the lucky contestants.

The Conserve Tuvs have made the giveaway program an instrument of national policy.

First they gave away offshore oil to Newfoundland.

Then they gave away onshore oil to the multi-nationals.

They gave away natural gas to the naturally gassy.

They gave away the Northwest Passage to the U.S. Coast Guard.

They gave away the fishing industry to the factory ships.

They gave away billions of dollars to the failed banks and their foreign depositors.

They gave away book publishing to Gulf and Western.

They gave away de Havilland to Boeing.

And the giveaway goes on.

So what's next, you say? Well, now that the Conserve Tuvs are talking free trade with the Americans, they'll end up giving away the rest of Canada.

85

The Jeer Leaders

Lately women have had to pinch themselves to make sure that it's not all a dream.

During the last Federal election campaign they were really impressed with the way that all three major parties *insisted* on putting women's issues on the front burner. That was political overkill, of course. Women would have been satisfied to see their issues *anywhere* on the stove, never mind the front burner. Until then women had only been able to get close enough to the stove to cook dinner.

During the Great TV Debates the three party leaders practically fell over backwards adding up all the things they were going to do for women after they got elected: wall-to-wall day care centres, equal pay for work of equal value, transition homes for battered women on every street corner, more rape crisis centres to keep pace with more rape, two Mother's Days a year, you name it. Nothing was too good for the little woman. All she had to do was put her cross on the ballot and the goodies would follow as the night the day.

Well, women thought, with a scenario like that, what's to lose? Of course, if they had been on their toes they would have smelled a rat, several in fact, but it did feel nice and warm being on the front burner for a change. Maybe at last women would come in out of the cold. Maybe the leopard *had* changed his spots. Maybe . . . It was the triumph of hope over experience.

The first inkling that something had gone wrong started to inkle when then Justice Minister Crosbie called the Honorable Member from Hamilton East "baby" in the House and the Government benches—male *and* female—burst into laughter. Then, to prove that nobody could outdo John Crosbie but John Crosbie himself, when the highly indignant member assured him that she was nobody's baby, least of all his, the Justice Minister called her a little wren, thereby demonstrating to the House the difference between patronage and patronizing. The government benches laughed on cue.

Then, one by one, the golden promises turned to lead. First, the Treasury Board was asked to examine the concept of equal work/equal pay in the civil service. Best estimates are that two years will be needed to produce a report which the government could then shelve.

Next, a parliamentary task force on child care was set up—but without either members or terms of reference; after all, important concerns are not to be hurried. Besides, if you wait long enough, the kids will have grown up.

Meantime, the government showed its support in principle by setting up a day care centre for wee Nicolas, the latest Mulroney, in Mila's suite of offices across the street from Parliament Hill. A small start, yes, but everyone knows that you have to crawl before you walk, particularly in a day care centre.

The final torpedo to women's hopes for a change in attitudes was delivered when a Yellowknife court convicted the Conserve Tuv member for the riding of Arctic Circle on a charge of wife-battering. Mr. Mulroney, mindful of his legal training, refused to comment on the case and the propriety of the member's retaining his seat on the ground that the matter was before the courts until the thirty-day appeal period had elapsed.

Now that women have pinched themselves awake they can see what became of the Prime Minister's promise of jobs, jobs, jobs. When the rhetoric and the chips were down it turned out to be slobs, slobs, slobs.

I Shot an Arrow

Fear of flyin'? Aye ma'am, that's always been the big Conserve Tuv hang-up. Their prime ministers all had white knuckles from Sir John, Eh? right on down.

'Course they didn't have aircraft in Sir John, Eh?'s time, y'know, but he was usually flyin' anyway. Didn't need a plane. Got his white knuckles from holdin' on to the whisky bottle too tight. Thought it might get away. Meanin' no offence, ma'am.

Then there was Dief. The Chief. Claimed the Avro Arrow made him giddy. Went too fast for a man from Prince Albert, eh? So he killed it. Sweetest little plane this side o' Kitty Hawk, too.

Times change, but not Conserve Tuvs. Those fine folks over at de Havilland spent 'bout a zillion of our dollars buildin' the Dash 8, but Mr. Mulroney, he didn't like the plane, ma'am. So he shot it down.

Boeing! Boeing!

Sire, the People are Revolting —as Usual

Marie Antoinette was absolutely right on that sunny July 14th morning. Trouble is, historians are still arguing about what she said.

The story is well known. When informed that the French Revolution was due to start at 2:15 that afternoon because the people had no bread she replied, with the logic that has marked French thought since the time of Descartes: "No bread? Let them eat cake."

Or did she?

To begin with, for two hundred years posterity has disagreed about what kind of cake. Bonaparte always insisted that what she had really said was: "Let them eat *napoléons*," a confection made of layers of puff pastry interlaid with a cream filling. He used the story that the Bourbon monarchy intended to eat him up in order to justify seizing power.

Proust, on the other hand, was just as certain that Marie had said: "Let them eat *madeleines*" as she dunked one of those little shell-shaped biscuits from Fauchon in her cuppa. Nor have other interpretations been lacking. Chairman Mao stated in his Little Red Book that what the queen had said was: "Let them eat fortune cookies."

Closer to home, Prime Minister Mulroney has added a new twist to the old story. A recent editorial charges him with having frittered away the biggest mandate in Canajan history, but the P.M. remains unrepentant.

Cake, you say? Never in Baie Comeau. What the P.M. actually said was: "Let them eat fritters."

The Watchdog Dogged Again

Quis custodiet ipsos custodes? That's what Horace used to ask Virgil as they sat sipping martinis and watching the evening sun go down behind the Seven Hills. Or as we non-Romans say: Who will take care of the caretaker's daughter while the caretaker's busy taking care? That old question surfaced in the House of Commons recently when Mr. Squeaky Clean himself, a.k.a. Erik Nielsen, was caught listening at the keyhole of the Grits' caucus room some twenty years ago. The resultant indignation among Honorable Members could be heard from Bella Coola, B.C. to the Straits of Belial.

It seems that although the Good Fairy in attendance at Erik's birth endowed him with Velcro lips she neglected to do the same for his ears which picked up, to quote him, "every bloody word" the Liberals said in caucus.

While Mr. Mulroney pooh-poohed the idea of any wrongdoing, other M.P.s felt that what may be good enough for a pooh-pooh artist like Mr. Mulroney won't do when the honor of Parliament is at stake.

The P.M., putting an arm around his colleague's shoulder reminded the House in moving terms of Mr. Nielsen's illustrious war record and his many years of devoted public service. Opposition members recalled, however, how Yukon Erik had high-sticked his way around the House of Commons for twenty years, indiscriminately spearing, butt-ending, tripping, kneeing, elbowing, board-checking, slashing and garotting his political opponents.

When then Justice Minster John Crosbie admitted that he would have done the same thing himself, the entire Opposition to a man, or at least to a man and woman, demanded that Mr. Nielsen apologize to the Canajan people.

After a very long weekend during which the Conserve Tuvs boned up on crisis management, Mr. Nielsen rose in the House all meek and mild to deliver an approximate apology.

In closing the debate, Mr. Mulroney asked the country to remember that Erik Nielsen is only human. That was asking a lot.

I ♥ Michael Wilson

Not since Edgar Benson, pipe tucked firmly into the corner of his chubby jaw, puffed his way into the hearts of Canajan taxpayers has so much love surrounded the Finance Ministry.

Michael Wilson is his own best witness to that.

When asked by reporters recently how Canajans felt about the way he is handling the economy, the Finance Minister replied: "They are saying, 'Thank you, Michael Wilson, thank you very much for everything you have done. You're on the right track, keep going.' " Even normally skeptical reporters were impressed by how the country was loving his tougher-than-tough fiscal measures.

Mr. Wilson is indeed on the right track and the outpouring of affection inspired by his policies has been nothing short of phenomenal, given the well-known reserve of most Canajans.

First there was the quite touching gratitude of the elderly at the prospect of having their pensions de-indexed for inflation. When Mr. Wilson told them how eager they were to help bring down the deficit they cheered him to the rafters. Oh, a few spoil-sports crabbed about it, but every politician knows that you can't please all of the people all of the time, which is why so few of them ever try.

Then when Mr. Wilson announced plans to de-index family allowances tear-stained letters of love poured in from all over the country. Whenever Mr. Wilson drove by in his black limo mothers held up little children to wave fondly at their benefactor. Even hardened media snobs were moved.

Mr. Wilson's staff, thinking to cash in on all this love and affection, organized a demo on Parliament Hill. They invited the Friends of Erik Nielsen and Marching Band to lead the parade, but, unfortunately, one member was in bed with a bad cold and the other member didn't want to march alone. To replace them the PMO co-opted the Bytown Sanitary Engineers Tuba Corps who oompah-pah'd their way along Wellington Street at the head of a platoon of widows and orphans carrying banners (in both official languages) reading "I LIKE MIKE!" on one side and, on the reverse, "J'AIME DES FLOCONS DE MAIS!" Turns out the banners were left over from the last Mike Pearson campaign when the Grits swept the country on the issue of bilingual cornflakes. Public Works just never throws anything out.

Prime Minister Mulroney announced to cheering crowds that Mr. Wilson deserved a gold medal for helping Canajans who couldn't help themselves. He may be right at that. As a symbol for the 1980s, Mike Wilson with a gold medal on his pin-striped chest sure beats Edgar Benson sucking on that old pipe.

Mulroney's Mistake

The Prime Minister is puzzled and who can blame him? When he started in public life Mr. Mulroney vowed to be as unlike Pierre Trudeau as possible and he kept his word. He didn't shrug. He didn't pirouette behind the Queen's back. He didn't tell striking truckdrivers what to eat. He didn't walk contemptuously among ordinary mortals with a rose in his buttonhole and a finger in the air.

That's because, unlike Pierre, Brian *wanted* to be liked. When he was a '*tit gars* in Baie Comeau the future P.M. had been told that by winning friends he could influence people. And it worked. From '*tit gars* to truckdriver (no one told *him* what to eat), from successful lawyer to iron ore magnate, from millionaire to Conserve Tuv leader, from Prime Minister to who knows what—Pope, maybe? Brian's path was positively littered with friends. He reached the top by pleasing people.

Now Brian is baffled. It seems the harder he tries to please Canajans the less pleased they become. People who used to say that he would still be P.M. in the year 2000 have started calling him a one-term Prime Minister. How could this happen?

Sir John, Eh? could have told him. John Diefenbaker could have told him. Mike Pearson could have told him. Even Joe Clark could have told him. So let's us tell him.

The truth is that Canajans cannot, will not, dare not be pleased. That's the rule of the road and politicians disregard it at their peril.

Think a moment. When our dollar was at U.S. $1.01, were Canajans pleased? They were not. Said it made our exports too dear. When the dollar fell to sixty-nine point something cents, were Canajans pleased? No way. Said it made our imports too dear.

When Sir John, Eh? built the transcontinental railway were Canajans pleased? Not bloody likely. Said it frightened the horses. When the government started shutting down one rail line after another were Canajans pleased? Are you kidding? Said they missed the train whistles at night.

And so it goes. Everybody knows that the surest way of getting Canajans' backs up is by trying to please them.

So Brian, knock it off, eh? Please Canajans? It can't be done.

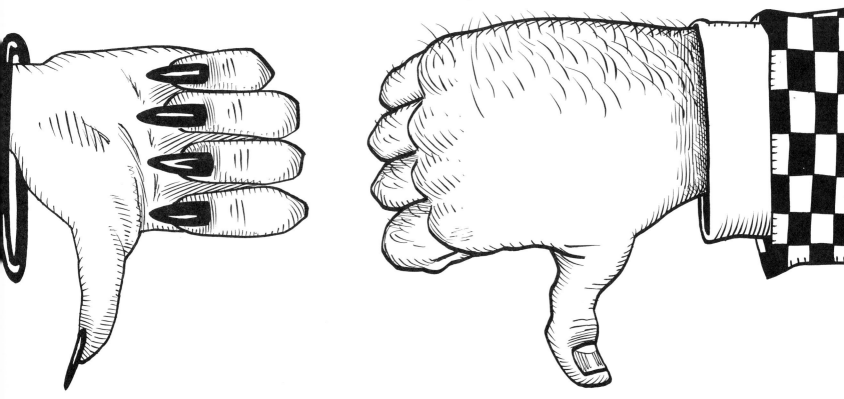